Big business among the stars leads to crime – and the Earth's Sun is stolen. While trying to get it back, Professor Gamma plays a very strange game of football...

Titles in Series 823

First edition

THE GIANTS OF UNIVERSAL PARK

by Fred and Geoffrey Hoyle
illustrated by Martin Aitchison

Ladybird Books Loughborough

The Giants of Universal Park

William had a half holiday from school, because there was to be an eclipse of the Sun. His science master had explained that eclipses take place because from time to time the Moon comes exactly between the Sun and the Earth and cuts off all the sunlight. It only stays a short while in this position, and in this eclipse it would only stay there for about a minute and a half, William had been told.

Many of William's fellow pupils had joined a specially organised school outing, which was to go to a hilltop thirty kilometres away to view the eclipse. William had decided to go his own way, however, and he was going fishing in the river that ran through the big estate close by William's home village.

The great thing was that, when the Sun's light became dimmed by the eclipse, William's enemy, Foxy the gamekeeper, wouldn't be able to see what was going on. Foxy was always on the prowl for poachers from the village, but this would be literally a "heaven-sent" opportunity to give him the slip.

So, collecting his somewhat makeshift fishing tackle from the garden shed, William made his way stealthily across the fields to the bushes that grew along the river bank. He was working his way slowly and quietly through the bushes when a voice made him freeze in his tracks.

"Hello there," it said.

William looked round to see the big shaggy form of his friend, Professor Gamma. Professor Gamma lived

with his young daughter, Kiryl, in an old house called Wit's End, deep inside a thick wood of very old yew trees on the flank of the broad low hill, the Down, that rose behind William's home village.

William hadn't noticed Gamma, because the Professor was well camouflaged. He was wearing green clothes that matched the foliage exactly, and today his hair was green as well, so that unless you spotted the purple colour of his face there really wasn't very much of him to be seen.

"We seem to be of like mind, young fellow. I thought I might do a bit of fishing too," said Gamma as William came up beside him.

It wasn't at all obvious how the Professor was going to do any fishing, for he seemed to have no tackle with him. However, once they reached the river bank itself, Gamma gave a quick twist to the walking stick he was carrying, which turned out to be hollow. From inside it he shook out two pieces of a rod, which, together with the stick itself, made up into a good-sized length when all three were clipped together. Then from a pocket of his green jacket, Gamma pulled out a reel and line which he proceeded to fit to the rod. William couldn't quite see how he made all the adjustments, but everything came together in a workmanlike way.

Lastly, the Professor took a flat box from inside his jacket. It contained a collection of flies, from which he chose a particular one with the greatest of care. Noticing William's bait – a jar of maggots – Gamma shook his head vigorously, so that his green hair waved about in the breeze.

"No, no!" he exclaimed. "Maggots would never do. We must conduct our poaching in a proper style."

The Professor then cast his fly in a long arc into the centre of the gently flowing river. As he did so, there was a loud creaking noise from his spine. It was something that often seemed to happen when Gamma made a sudden movement. At first the creaking noise had surprised William, but by now he was used to it. Today however he was worried in case Foxy should hear it.

During the next hour the Professor landed three trout, each quite large. William was so occupied in watching the flick of Gamma's line, and in keeping a sharp look-out for Foxy the gamekeeper, that he quite forgot about the eclipse. It was only when he heard the birds begin to twitter everywhere among the bushes that he remembered it. The science master at school had said that the birds would make quite a noise, and as the sunlight quickly faded, that was just what they did.

William had been told to look carefully for the pearly-white light of the corona which surrounds the Sun, but try as he would he could see nothing at all at the place where the Sun had been a minute or two before. The sky there was a complete blank. In other places there were the usual stars, exactly the way they are seen at night.

"This eclipse seems to be going on for a very long time," grunted Gamma from close by.

William was not very good at judging time, but certainly the blackness seemed to have lasted for much more than a minute and a half.

"Why would that be?" he asked.

"It looks to me like dirty work at the crossroads," the Professor replied.

William was just about to ask what he meant, when he heard somebody pushing through the bushes towards them, breathing hard. The thought of Foxy naturally entered William's head, but Foxy certainly wouldn't be running hard along the river bank in such a faint light as this, a light coming only from the stars.

The panting was quite loud now. Then a voice said, almost in William's ear, "Something's wrong. I think it may be quite serious!"

It was Kiryl, the Professor's daughter.

"There's something much bigger than the Moon in front of the Sun," Kiryl went on. "You can see it for yourself," she added to her father, handing him what looked to William like a pair of binoculars. Gamma lifted the binoculars and studied for a long time the part of the sky where the sun should have been. William didn't understand why Gamma and Kiryl needed binoculars, for he could easily see with his own eyes that there was a great black patch in the sky where the Sun ought to have been. Nor did he understand the Professor's next remark: "I don't like the look of this one little bit. It looks uncommonly like my old friend Lighto's work."

Through the gloom, William saw the Professor produce his pipe from his jacket pocket. There was a sudden flare as Gamma struck a match to light it and began to puff away. As William knew from past experience, this meant action, for the pipe was an energy pipe – a communications switch to the pathways that criss-cross the whole Universe.

The glow in the bowl of the pipe gradually grew brighter and brighter, until the surrounding bushes and the nearby reaches of the river were all bathed in a red glow. This was the moment before dematerialisation. William never cared twopence about dematerialising. It was the thought of

materialising again that always worried him, because you had to be careful that it happened in a proper way. It was no good at all if your head materialised in England and your body in Australia!

There was a brilliant flash, then William felt a sudden surge of speed, from which he knew they had joined the local pathway that led from the Solar System out into the complex maze of routes along the Milky Way – and far outside it too, if that was where you wanted to be.

"We'll take a quick look around before we get far out from Earth," Gamma said.

They did a quick loop towards Mars and Jupiter, and an amazing sight met their eyes. Two glowing clouds in space had the shapes of giant figures. The body of one of them was shielding the Earth from the Sun.

"So that's why the Sun disappeared," remarked Kiryl.

"I think we're just in time to see a most serious crime being committed," her father answered.

William watched in astonishment as the great hand of one of the figures wound itself into a throwing action, like a pitcher in the game of baseball. Then came the throw as the figure unwound, and a blazing white object emerged from its hand. Instantly, the voice of Gamma boomed out loudly, so loudly that it echoed out and re-echoed everywhere throughout the energy pathway.

"Thieves!" he yelled. "Thieves! They're stealing our Sun."

No sooner were the words out of the Professor's mouth than the two giant figures streaked off at enormous speed after the Sun which they had thrown clean out of the Solar System.

"This is going to cause real trouble," muttered Gamma, clenching the big pipe tightly between his teeth.

William watched as they came with an enormous cascade of sparks into the general maze of universal pathways. It was like being on an express train racing across a vast railway yard, with junction points everywhere around them. Every time they crossed a junction there was a big flash of blue light from the Professor's pipe.

"No time to lose," grunted Gamma by way of explanation.

Fast as they were going, the two giants ahead of them were going just as fast, and ahead of the giants there was a much smaller white ball, which William realised must be the Sun.

"Professional thieves!" grunted Gamma again.

"But who are they?" William asked.

"The sons of Lighto. Who else? Trained as thieves from birth," was the answer.

"But what do they want with our Sun?" William persisted.

"Lighto will have a buyer for it. Never steals stars on spec. Too risky. Too easily seen and too hot to store away," the Professor told him.

Although they were not catching up on the two star-thieves, the white ball ahead was growing steadily bigger, so that William knew they must be catching up on the Sun itself.

"They didn't throw it hard enough," said Kiryl.

"We're on the upper-energy side of it," agreed the Professor, still gritting his teeth on the pipe.

Something quite amazing then happened. One of the gigantic star-thieves changed shape. The head, body, arms and legs all disappeared, to be replaced by a completely new shape. William could hardly believe it, and he rubbed his eyes and looked again. The shape was that of a huge gleaming boot! The boot surged forward until the toe kicked the white ball of the Sun. The Sun instantly took off at a greatly increased speed, so fast that instead of catching up with it, as they had been doing before, the white ball now grew smaller and smaller as it receded from them.

"Alley brats! They've got every trick in the book," shouted Gamma, in a voice so loud that William thought it must be heard half-way across the galaxy.

Their speed increased, so much so that Kiryl exclaimed anxiously, "Father! Don't forget what happened the last time you went as fast as this."

"Can't worry about that! Unless we get a move on, the Earth is going to experience dramatic changes," the Professor replied as the space time warp around them became more and more extreme.

What looked like an enormous volcanic eruption of flashes, flames and sparks burst out ahead of them. The two star-thieves became illuminated in the outburst as if light were shining through their bodies, which seemed to be made of diffuse white plastic.

"Serves them right! There's justice for you!" roared the Professor in the greatest glee.

"Look out!" yelled Kiryl, but too late.

It was like a skier racing at a furious pace onto a mass of great boulders. One moment they were running smoothly and the next they were flying in all directions, completely out of control. It was a magnetic field, interwoven like the thread of a piece of cloth, that ran directly at right angles to their path.

William lost all sense of shape. First he seemed to be a long cigar, then a rapidly pulsating sphere. Then once the sphere stopped its swellings and contractions it started to send out sharp spikes in one direction after another. There was nothing for it but to let himself go, and he bounced along, enveloped in a halo of blue flame.

Just as William was thinking that this was surely the end of him, a gruff voice sounded loudly in his ear. To his surprise it said, "Ticket!"

"What ticket?" William somehow managed to ask.

"Don't think you're going to get away with that, my lad! I've had people trying to bounce their way in here before," the voice replied.

William waited a moment, and he gradually came to his senses. Then he realised that he had materialised, and was standing on an open platform.

"Professor Gamma!" he shouted.

"Does he have tickets?" the gruff voice asked.

"Yes," replied William. "That's why I'm calling him."

"So long as he has tickets, that'll be all right then. But nobody's bouncing past me into Universal Park."

After all the bright flashes and sparks, William had not at first been able to make out much in the faint light on the platform, but now that his eyes were becoming adapted to the dark he could see better again. Ahead of him was a high barrier, except where a glow of light emerged through a passageway of some kind. The trouble was that, directly in front of the

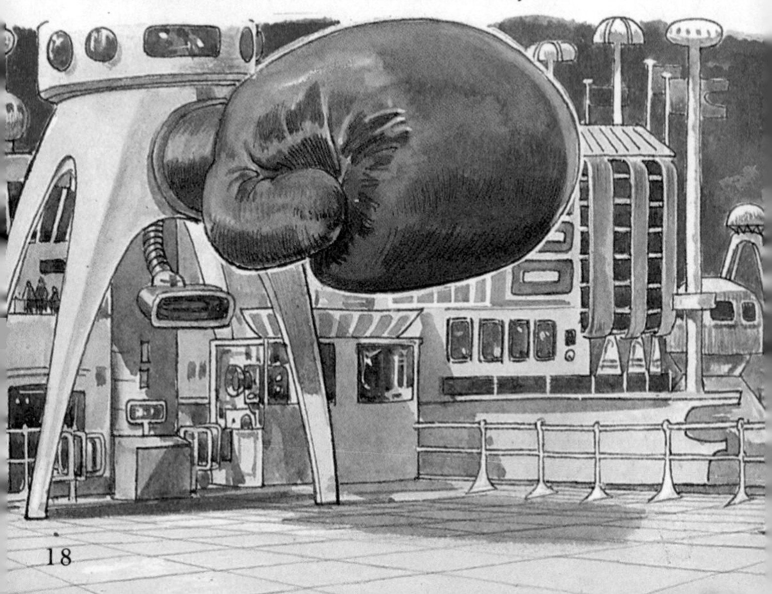

passageway, a colossal fist wearing what looked like a still more enormous boxing glove guarded the entrance to the passageway. William had a feeling that when he'd materialised he must have run slap-bang into that tremendous fist.

It was then that William noticed Kiryl, lying on the far side of the platform. He went quickly to her, and as he knelt down beside her, she opened her eyes and said in a low voice, "I'm trying to recover, but I'm dreadfully bruised and my head aches. I'm sure I must have run straight into that fist thing over there."

"So did I," answered William sympathetically, "and I'm still trying to get back again to my proper shape."

As Kiryl climbed slowly to her feet, a short sharp whistle from nearby caused them both to turn quickly. A man no bigger than William was standing there. He was dressed in a suit made out of yellow, red and blue

patches of material, and around his neck and most of his head was a long scarf. In fact there was little to be seen of his features except the mouth and eyes.

"Psst!" the fellow whistled quickly. "You want tickets?"

"What would we want tickets for?" Kiryl asked, puzzled.

"For the big game, of course, Dynamos versus Magnetics. Game of the year."

William had heard of ticket scalpers, and he knew they always wanted a lot of money, which he and Kiryl didn't have. He was just about to say so when the little man stepped forward and took something from William's hand. It was his old fishing tackle, which William had been clutching in the moment back on Earth when they'd dematerialised.

"A nice antique," said the man approvingly. "Don't find 'em like this nowadays. Worth quite a lot I should think."

In return the man handed William two cards with a lot of holes punched in them. The only words on the cards read: Dynamo Light versus Real Magnetism.

William was just on the point of thanking the fellow for the tickets when the strange scarf-swaddled figure said, "Actually, I was told to give 'em to you. By a geezer with a big pipe and a purple face. But I'll keep this antique all the same. Should fetch a bit, like I said."

The three of them walked over the platform to where the fist was guarding the passageway. William was walking right up to it when the little man grabbed him tightly by the arm, saying, "Hey, hey! It'll knock you into kingdom-come if you go too close."

As if to emphasise this opinion, a voice from the fist shouted, "Tickets! Nobody bounces past me."

"But if I don't go up to it, how can I hand over the tickets?" William asked.

"Fancy not knowing that! Where on earth were you born?" the little man wanted to know.

He grabbed the cards out of William's hand and then simply flung them at the enormous fist. Immediately the cards were thrown there was a loud sucking noise, as if a giant vacuum cleaner had been switched on. In a quick swirl the tickets disappeared, and across the big boxing-glove face of the fist, numbers and words began to flash, as William had seen them do on a television screen.

"Checking up on you," the little man explained.

A moment later, the fist withdrew with a loud plop into a space that opened beside the passageway through the barrier. A small shining sphere emerged and waited, hovering. The glove thumb pointed at it and said in a voice rather less gruff than before, "Your guide – follow it."

"Off you go," nodded the little man, from deeper inside his scarf.

"Are you coming with us?" asked Kiryl.

"Not on your life, I've got my own special ways into places like this."

With a further couple of twirls of the scarf the little man's face disappeared even more completely. He gave a final nod towards William and said, "See you later, gladiator!"

A second later and he was gone.

The little sphere led Kiryl and William upwards through the passageway. It was really an ascending tunnel through the barrier that enclosed a vast stadium, Universal Park, as the gruff voice had said. Inside the stadium, the light was so bright that for a moment it dazzled them completely. The sphere paused when they paused, so that Kiryl and William were able to stop and take a quick look round.

The light was coming from six stars, one at each corner of the rectangular stadium and two half-way along the bigger sides of the rectangle. Kiryl pointed towards one of these two. "That's our Sun," she said. "Now I see why they wanted it. To light the stadium."

"How do you know it's our Sun?" William asked.

"Because it's got exactly the same spots on it as it had before it was stolen."

Kiryl handed William a piece of old exposed film which she had taken from a pocket. He held it up to his eyes and was able to look through it straight at the Sun. Sure enough, there were spots, but since William didn't know what the sunspots had been like before, he had to take Kiryl's word for it.

William had expected the stadium to be full, but he hadn't expected to find it filled in such a peculiar way, for on one side of the rectangle it was packed with giants and on the other side it was chock-a-block with dwarfs. Nor had William expected quite such a dreadful noise. The huge number of dwarfs that packed the stands towards which the little sphere was guiding them were all shouting and singing, while the giants on the other side of the stadium were blowing on hunting horns all the time. Everywhere in the giant-stand bright metal reflected the lights. The giants were wearing helmets as well as carrying hunting horns. To William, they looked for all the world like an enormous horde of Vikings.

At last the guiding sphere arrived at two seats. William had thought that Gamma would be there, but the Professor was not to be seen. William was a bit worried about this, but when he mentioned it to Kiryl she simply shrugged and said, "Oh, he'll be up to one of his tricks. You can be sure of that."

Now he was seated amongst them, William could see the dwarfs weren't dwarfs really. It was just that they looked dwarfs in comparison with the giants who were still thunderously blowing away on their horns on the opposite side of the big rectangular area on which the game, William supposed, was soon to be played.

In fact, the dwarfs were no smaller than William. They were just like the man who had given them the tickets, and they all wore jackets made out of yellow, red and blue patches. The only difference was that the people here in the stands were all wearing tam-o'-shanters. Kiryl said they looked much too big for them, because the tam-o'-shanters sat well down over their heads.

One of the two teams began to emerge into the arena. Instead of appearing all together, as William had seen them do in soccer matches, they appeared one by one, and as they did so there was an announcement of their identity on a loudspeaker system, which was so very loud that it could even be heard above the massed braying of horns on the far side of the arena.

The players of this first side were all of giant size, and they all appeared in the same style, with a springing, prancing run, and with their chests puffed out like enormous pigeons. As each one came on to the field, there were boos and cat calls from the crowd around William and Kiryl. To avoid seeming different, they joined in the boos and cat calls.

Then it was the turn of the second team, who looked like minute dwarfs compared to the first team, although William knew by now that the dwarfs were really as big as he was. The dwarfs were greeted by rapturous applause from the surrounding crowd who roared, "Come on, the glory boys. Come on, the clever boys. M-A-G-N-E-T-I-C-S!"

So the dwarfs were the Real Magnetics, and the giants were the Dynamo Lights, William worked out. But neither William nor Kiryl could see how such tiny fellows could possibly compete with such big ones. Surely it was going to be an easy victory for the Dynamo Lights!

Unlike the Dynamo Lights who had emerged player by player, the Magnetics appeared in a bunch all together, and every one was wearing a tam-o'-shanter down to his ears, just like the crowd. And like the crowd they wore shirts made out of yellow, red and blue patches.

The Dynamos took the half of the arena to the right, and the Magnetics the half to the left. William could now see a structure at each end of the arena which he thought must be the two goals. But instead of goal posts there was a bright half-circular ring of light to mark the goal area, and instead of a back-netting to the goal, there was a quarter-sphere of clear plastic.

No sooner were the Magnetics in position on their side of the arena than they all threw their tam-o'-shanters high in the air. To William's astonishment the tam-o'-shanters all exploded with sharp cracking noises, and since each exploded at a slightly different instant, it was just like an enormous firework going off. The crowd around William and Kiryl roared its approval at this performance, whereas the giants opposite blew great rasping sounds on their horns.

Fascinating as this might be, William was still more fascinated by the referee. It was simply a huge whistle!

Instead of running about the field like a human referee, the whistle glided smoothly and with great speed around the arena. The ball was a sphere of light, much bigger and brighter than the sphere which had guided Kiryl and William to their seats, but otherwise much the same.

"The game will begin," a voice suddenly announced. The whistle turned bright red for a moment, then blew a shrill piercing blast. Immediately, one of the giants on the right began to run with a springing, prancing motion towards the sphere of light, which had been placed in the very centre of the arena.

While ten paces from the sphere, the giant began to change shape. At first, William couldn't tell what the new shape was going to be, but by the time it reached the sphere the shape had become a boot. This was not too much of a surprise to William because this was just the way the Sun had been stolen. What was really surprising was that the bright sphere, instead of remaining a round ball, became converted into a beam of light that darted into the Magnetic half of the arena, directed straight for the goal on William's left.

"Great scattering of light by light," the announcer boomed.

"Rubbish!" shouted the crowd around William and Kiryl, derisively.

One of the defending Magnetics leapt upwards to intercept the darting beam of light. It was surprising how high the little chap was able to jump. Much more surprising, however, was that just before making the interception, the defender disappeared entirely.

The beam was deflected towards a second defender, who also disappeared just at the moment that the beam reached him. Immediately, the beam was darting back towards the giants on the right-hand side of the arena. Both the defenders then reappeared!

"Great deflections by black holes 3 and 9," boomed an announcer, at which remark there were loud rasping sounds from the Viking horns on the far side of the arena.

"I think that must be it," whispered Kiryl in William's ear. "The Magnetics deflect the beam by making themselves into black holes, whereas the giants kick it by using the scattering of light by light." William didn't quite understand this, but he nodded intelligently.

William had quite lost count of the many times the beam of light had been kicked by the giants and deflected by the dwarfs, when a kick by the giants, coming from an unusual angle, evaded all the dwarfs. Several of the dwarfs leapt in vain attempts to intercept it, disappearing as usual and then reappearing when they fell back onto the floor of the arena.

The beam of light entered the goal of the Magnetics, and a flame instantly burst from the quarter-sphere at the back of it. In the cacophony from the opposite side of the arena there was now a deeper boom, coming from much bigger instruments which had exceedingly long mouthpieces, like Alpine horns.

This was not all, for in front of the Dynamo stand there appeared a blazing spiral whirl of light. It rolled along what would have been called the touchline in a game of football. The blazing spiral rolled on and on, so that pretty soon it became clear that it was going to roll right round the whole arena. Long before it reached the place where Kiryl and William were sitting

they could feel a great heat coming from the thing.

It was then that everybody in the surrounding crowd whipped off their tam-o'-shanters. William felt a tap on his shoulder. Turning, he saw the little man who had provided them with the tickets sitting immediately behind. The man handed William two tam-o'-shanters saying, "Exchanged the antique for 'em."

William was on the point of thanking him, when the fellow added, "Better get into shelter."

Everybody around was sheltering under a tam-o'-shanter, so William and Kiryl did exactly the same as the others were doing. Even so, they could feel a fiery breath sweep over the stand as the flaming spiral rolled by along the touchline below them.

William turned to find the little man now standing. "Well, that's that, that is," he said cheerfully, and with a knowing wink at William he added, "See you soon, Half-a-Moon." Then he was gone.

The whistle blew for the game to start again. No sooner was the beam of light darting again back and forth between the giants and the dwarfs than the crowd around Kiryl and William began a persistent chant. "Dispersion! Dispersion! We want dispersion!" they yelled.

Suddenly, at a deflection by one of the dwarfs, the

single white beam split into two coloured beams. "That's the idea! Give it to 'em, boys," yelled the crowd in delight.

At each further deflection, the coloured beams split into more and more beams, until the Magnetics had the whole Dynamo team desperately booting away at one or another of them. Whenever the beams split, new colours always emerged, until the arena below looked as bright as a flower show. As the beams multiplied, the Dynamos became more and more confused. Then suddenly the beams all converged together at a point not far from the Dynamo goal. At just the correct position to receive them was a Magnetics player. As he deflected the many beams, with the usual disappearing and reappearing act, all the diverse colours came together again into a single white beam that darted instantly into the Dynamo goal entrance. A huge flame spurted from the quarter-sphere behind the goal.

The crowd around Kiryl and William roared in an ecstasy of delight, and for the first time since they'd entered the stadium, the braying horns in the Dynamo stand were silent. On the loudspeaker system there was a cry of "Hey! Stop that!" from the announcer, followed by a strained gulping sound. Then a new voice could be heard, a voice so loud that it even silenced the roaring crowd.

"Thieves!" it thundered. "You have stolen the star belonging to a defenceless planet. For this you are liable to prosecution under Section H 9741 of the Code Universal, Star Subsection 5. Consider yourselves all to be under mandatory arrest."

"Oh dear! Now we are in for real trouble," groaned Kiryl. It was Professor Gamma!

After all the noise, the dead silence which now descended on the stadium was almost unbearable. It went on and on, second after second, until something just had to give. Suddenly, a single horn in the Dynamo stand made a rasping noise. It was instantly joined by a second, then a third and a fourth, until in much less time than it takes to tell, the rasping noise rose to a deafening volume.

Around William and Kiryl the crowd took up a chant again.

"Prove your point, sea lawyer! Prove your point!" it yelled, and then, "Show us your credentials!"

The voice of Gamma immediately took up the challenge. "My credentials," he said, "are that I will score a goal alone, against the combined forces of the Dynamo Lights and the Real Magnetics who – if I may say so – don't seem to know how this game should really be played."

"Why on earth does he have to say things like that?" groaned Kiryl.

The whistle started to blow furiously, sliding rapidly up and down the arena. William saw that it was directing the Dynamo players into the same half as the Magnetics, leaving the right side of the arena empty except for a small figure which appeared and took up a position in front of what had previously been the Dynamo goal. It was Professor Gamma.

Every one of the Dynamo players now changed into a boot. Not content with that, the boots started to join up one to another, growing in size as they did so, until eventually there was only one truly enormous boot.

"Unfair tactics!" yelled Kiryl, "Unfair tactics!"

"Whose side are you on?" the crowd roared at her.

The single great boot into which the Dynamo players had amalgamated themselves slid its way at great speed to where a new sphere of light was positioned at the centre of the arena.

The kick was far more ferocious than anything which William had yet seen, and the emerging beam of light seemed much bigger than before. It also seemed to move very fast indeed to where Gamma was waiting for it in front of the goal.

Both Kiryl and William fully expected the beam to go straight past the Professor. They both looked for the flame from the quarter-sphere that would signal a crushing defeat. But there was no flame. Somehow the Professor had managed to intercept the beam. This could be seen because, through intercepting it, Gamma was bowled head over heels. The impact almost carried him into the goal itself, but with a great effort he managed to stop the slide just short of the entrance area.

Gamma was now on his feet again, running towards the half of the arena where his opponents were enmassed. The strange thing was that the beam of light had disappeared completely.

"He's hiding it! Purple face is hiding it! Scrag him! Cream him! Bury him!" yelled the crowd in a frenzy.

William could see that the Professor's hand was steadying the pipe, which, as always, he still clenched in his teeth. As William watched, great clouds of smoke poured from the pipe. The wind carried the smoke towards the charging Magnetics and Dynamos. The Magnetics were nearer to Gamma, because the Dynamos had lost time in changing from the one single huge boot back to their individual prancing, running shapes. So the smoke hit the Magnetics first. It affected them like tear gas, causing their eyes to stream like rivers in flood.

More and more of the acrid smoke belched from Gamma's pipe. When it eventually reached the prancing Dynamos, who by now were breathing deeply as they ran, it hit them with racking coughs in their huge chests. As each of the Dynamo players coughed out the smoke which he had gulped, it formed into a large ring that rose high above the arena. Pretty soon, William could see a whole set of these smoke rings

billowing over the seething mass of players as they tried to grab hold of the Professor. But their efforts were quite in vain, because by now Gamma was entirely hidden in the smoke-screen which he had created.

To the spectators, it was rather like looking down on to black storm clouds. Every now and then there seemed to be a flash of lightning below the clouds. Suddenly, however, Gamma emerged from his smoke-screen at an open spot immediately in front of his opponents' goal. In the same instant, the beam of light blazed out from the bowl of his pipe, where – as William had long ago guessed – it had been trapped. The beam of light flashed into the goal, raising the usual huge flame from the quarter-sphere behind.

Gamma was not content with this, however. The first flash from the pipe was followed by a second, which also penetrated the goal, raising a still larger flame.

Then there was a third flash, then a fourth, then a fifth, in a series that seemed without end. These further beams crashed like thunder over the heads of the crowds in the stands. It was just about then that the smoke from the arena reached the stands where William and Kiryl were. Everyone's eyes began to water, just as had happened with the Magnetic players. And in the Dynamo stand, everybody started to cough and to blow smoke rings, just as the Dynamo players in the arena had done.

Somebody in the Dynamo stand tried to blow on a horn, but the hoot of it soon turned into a wail.

"Give the man his star back! Get old purple-face out of here! For Heaven's sake, get him out of here!" moaned the crowd around William and Kiryl.

William glanced to where the Sun was positioned as it illuminated the area. Even as he watched, a loud high-pitched whistle arose, and with it the brilliant light of the Sun began to dim.

"Your star is on its way home," yelled the crowd. "Now please get out, for pity's sake. Get out of here and leave us alone!"

As he heard the words "get out", a sense of extreme urgency swept through William. He knew he must find the Professor quickly. There was not a moment, an instant, to be lost. But how could he and Kiryl possibly find Gamma in the lurid turbulent sea of smoke which still filled the floor of the arena below them? That question seemed unanswerable.

Just then a voice said, "Psst!" It was the little man who had given them the tickets and the tam-o'-shanters. "We leave by the back door," he added, grabbing Kiryl and William each by an arm. Pulling them with him, the man launched himself through an opening into a smooth chute. It was a quick helter-skelter route down to the arena, where there was a vehicle rather like a Moon-rover waiting.

The little man leapt into the driver's seat, William jumped in beside him and Kiryl and the Professor wedged themselves in the back. The vehicle did not run like an ordinary vehicle, however, or even like a Moon-rover. It slid smoothly over the arena, skidding when they had to change direction, and skidding too to avoid the players. Although the little man really had enough to do in controlling the skids, he still managed to take a big silver badge from a pocket in his jacket. Flicking it under William's nose, he said proudly, "Galactic police!"

Seconds later, the vehicle swirled to a halt. Kiryl was first out of the vehicle. As William dismounted, the little man took him momentarily by the arm.

"May see you again, somewhere in the rain," he said, with another big wink. Then he was gone.

William was just about to ask the Professor what all the rush was about, when there was a brilliant flash that instantly dematerialised them for the return journey home. Even now, William couldn't get much of an explanation out of Gamma. All he said was, "We must get the Sun back, and in its own proper time."

It was just about the quickest, most breathless homeward trip William had ever made. All through the journey, they could see the Sun ahead of them, returning to the solar system. Only when Gamma was satisfied that the Sun had gone safely to its rightful place, did he give the signal for them to materialise.

William hit the bank of the river, at the place where he and Gamma had been fishing, with such a thump that it knocked the last bit of breath out of him. Kiryl too hit a thorn bush beside the river bank. The Professor had the worst landing, however, for with a mighty splash and a roar he materialised in the middle of the river, at the exact spot where he had been casting the fly with his rod.

Gulping and thrashing with his arms and feet, Gamma reached the river bank. William helped him out, nearly falling in himself in the process.

"Well, at least we've got both the Sun and ourselves back in the right places. The question now is whether we've returned in the right time," muttered the Professor, as he stood dripping from head to foot on the river bank. When William asked the meaning of this ominous remark, the Professor went on, "To tell you the honest truth, I don't know whether we've come back a thousand years in the future, or a thousand years in the past, or whether we're just right."

As he spoke, there was a loud angry shout, "I'll get you now, you poaching blighters! I'll soon have you!" It was Foxy the gamekeeper.

"I see we were exactly right in our timing!" grinned Gamma. "I also see that we had better be moving along, rapidly!"

With this the Professor took to his heels, with long raking strides that the gamekeeper had no hope of matching. As he raced away, William could hear the familiar sharp cracking noises from Gamma's spine. Since Kiryl also vanished completely into the bushes, it was after William that Foxy was now rushing.

In a race with Foxy, William always preferred to run over rough ground. It was best over a ploughed field. But now the field ahead was smooth. Partly because of this, and partly because he still hadn't got his breath back, William could hear the gamekeeper's pounding feet getting closer and closer. He was going to be caught! Unless . . .

There was just one hope. Ahead was a wooden fence. With a last furious effort William reached the fence and somehow managed to vault it. Because Foxy had to stop to climb instead of vaulting, this gave William the few seconds margin to reach the lane which led to his home. A moment later he was through the garden gate, and another moment later he was opening the back door of the house.

William's mother gave a little scream as he burst in through the door.

"What on earth are you doing in that awful tam-o'-shanter?" she asked in an astonished voice. When he reached his bedroom, William took a look at himself in a mirror. There, sure enough, was the large tam-o'-shanter which the little man had given him, so large that it was sitting heavily far down on his ears.

At dinner that night, William's father – who was an engineer – said, "The scientists are very puzzled about that eclipse this afternoon. Seems it lasted a lot longer than they'd expected, and they've all got egg on their faces."

"How do you mean?" asked William.

"He means they all got it wrong," explained his mother.

As soon as he could, William slipped away from the dinner table. Several minutes later his mother started to clear the dishes. On her second trip to the kitchen, she stopped by a window that overlooked the garden, and said in a low questioning voice, "I wonder why he's doing that?"

When her husband came over to the window, he could see that William was repeatedly tossing the large tam-o'-shanter high into the air.

"It would baffle the wisdom of Solomon to know what goes on in that boy's head," he remarked. Then, as he was walking back to his chair beside the fire, there came a sudden loud noise that made him jump.

Several sharp explosions seemed to be going off at slightly different moments. It sounded to William's father exactly like the explosion of a giant firework.